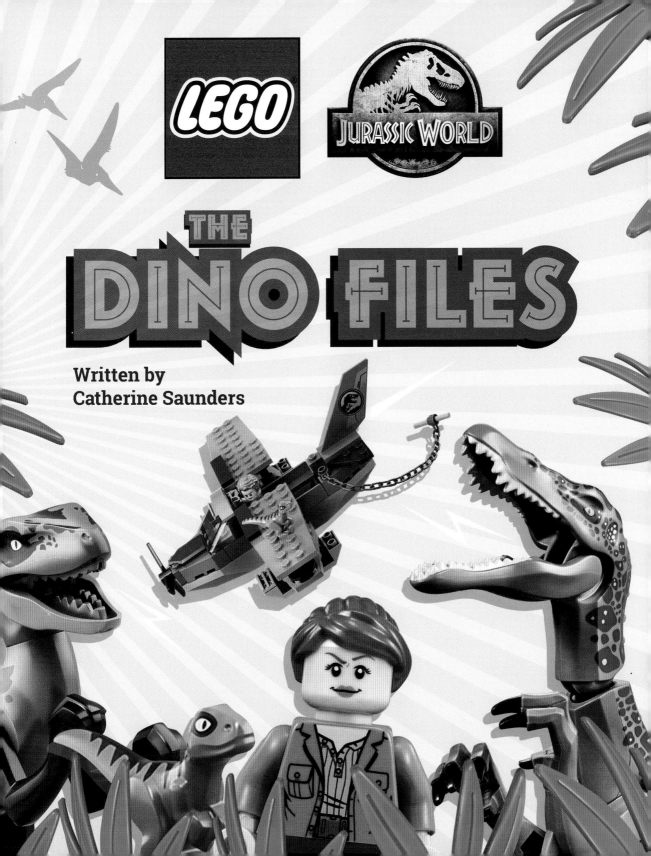

LEGO

JURASSIC WORLD

THE DINO FILES

Written by
Catherine Saunders

CONTENTS

WELCOME

LOOK OUT FOR THESE INCREDIBLE DINOS!

Dinosaurs are fascinating—what they looked like, how they moved, and what they ate. Imagine meeting a dinosaur in an amazing theme park. Now that would be awesome! It might be a little scary, too, but of course the theme park would have to be totally safe. It would be a fantastic idea—wouldn't it? Read on to find out more about Jurassic Park, and its successor, Jurassic World ...

DINO DATA

The Earth is super old. It formed about 4.6 billion years ago, and the first dinosaurs appeared just over 230 million years ago in the Mesozoic Era. In comparison, modern humans are practically babies. We have only been around for a mere 200,000 years!

The Mesozoic Era had three main periods—the **Triassic, Jurassic,** and **Cretaceous.**

Most of the things we know about dinosaurs comes from **fossils**—bits of bone, teeth, or traces (like footprints) preserved in rocks.

THERE'S STILL A LOT WE DON'T KNOW ABOUT DINOS!

Dinosaur fossils have been found **all over the world,** even in Antarctica.

Some dinosaurs are named after **who** found them; the **place** they were found; or an **important feature,** such as a horn.

Scientists have discovered about

1,500

different species of dinosaur so far, and on average, they discover a new one **every few weeks!**

DINOSAURS ARE MY FAVORITE ANIMALS.

Some dinosaurs were tiny. **Others were**

enormous.

Some dinosaurs ate **meat** (carnivores), some ate **plants** (herbivores), and some ate **both** (omnivores).

11

JURASSIC PARK

Most dinosaurs died out millions of years ago. But rich businessman John Hammond wants to give them a second chance. He has a team of scientists recreate a whole host of dinosaurs. Hammond plans to show off his creations in a specially built theme park. **Welcome to Jurassic Park!**

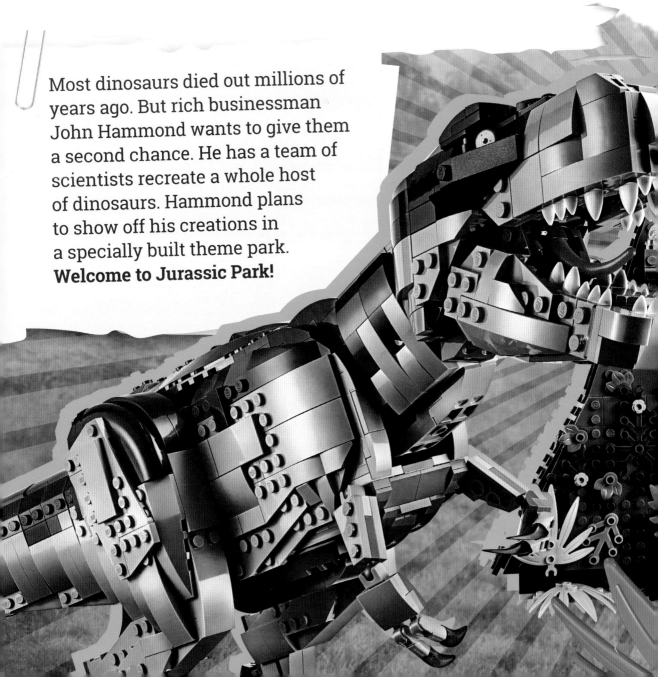

JOHN HAMMOND

Owner and creator of Jurassic Park

John Hammond is a successful businessman, and he invests his fortune in projects that interest him. He has founded animal parks around the world, but Jurassic Park is his most daring idea yet. He just hopes it works!

YOU'LL BE ASTONISHED BY WHAT WE HAVE CREATED!

Hammond is dressed for a jungle expedition.

Expert opinions

Hammond also shows the park to Dr. Alan Grant and Dr. Ellie Sattler before opening it. He hopes these scientific experts like his park.

Grandfather

Hammond invites his two grandchildren, Tim and Lex Murphy, to the park before it opens. He wants them to have a sneak peek!

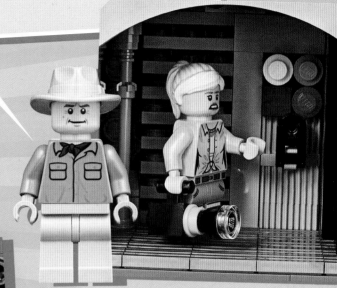

Fine dining

Hammond expects the best in all areas of his life. At the park, he has a private dining room where top chefs prepare his favorite meals.

Another expert

Math expert Dr. Ian Malcolm is invited to see the park, too. Malcolm thinks creating dinos in modern times is a bad idea. Hammond thinks he's wrong!

WHO'S WHO

John Hammond wants to show off Jurassic Park before it opens to the public. His grandchildren and the scientific experts he invited have all arrived. Hammond hopes that his talented and trusted staff will make everything run smoothly. He's sure that nothing can go wrong ...

DR. ALAN GRANT

*OH MY. IT'S AN ACTUAL **DINOSAUR!***

Job: Paleontologist

An expert in: Fossils and all things dino-related.

Likes: Writing books about dinosaurs. His hat.

DR. ELLIE SATTLER

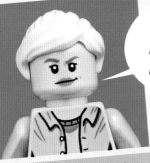

*THOSE PLANTS ARE **POISONOUS!***

Job: Paleobotanist

An expert in: plant fossils. They're amazing!

She would: Spot a plant and not see the big dino behind ...

DR. IAN MALCOLM

*LIFE WILL **ALWAYS** FIND A WAY.*

Job: Mathematician

An expert in: Chaos theory; patterns; being a know-it-all.

Believes that: Humans are not able to control dinos.

DR. HENRY WU

*IT'S **HATCHING** TIME, PEOPLE.*

Job: Lead genetic biologist

Creates: Dinosaurs in the park's high-tech laboratory.

Likes: Coffee; merrily ignoring danger; successful experiments.

DENNIS NEDRY

*NICE DINOSAUR. **FETCH!***

Job: Computer programmer

Most likely to: Steal dino DNA; accidentally let dinos loose.

Least likely to: Make friends with a *Dilophosaurus*.

TIM MURPHY

DINOSAURS ARE AWESOME!

Age: 8

Likes: Dinosaurs; reading Dr. Alan Grant's books.

Dislikes: Being chased by a *T. rex* or attacked by *Raptors*.

LEX MURPHY

LET'S GO, LITTLE BROTHER!

Age: 12

Skills: Using, fixing, or hacking into computers.

Likes: Vegetarian food; visiting her grandfather.

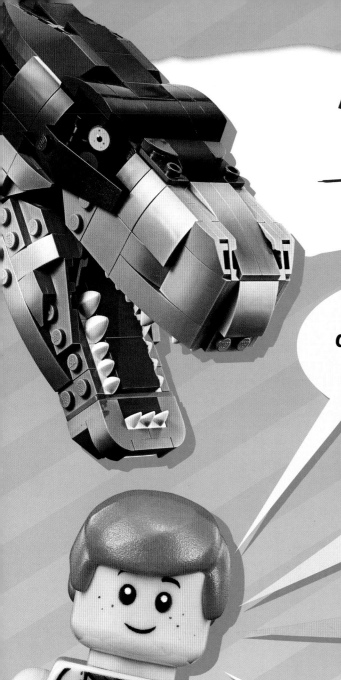

ASK THE EXPERT

Tim Murphy asks Dr. Alan Grant some important questions

Q: What were dinosaurs and how did they move?

Q: Which dinosaur was the biggest?

Q: How do you know so much about dinosaurs?

Q: What happened to the dinosaurs?

A: Dinosaurs were reptiles, like lizards, crocodiles, and snakes. Some dinosaurs walked on two legs; others on four legs. Some dinosaurs were excellent swimmers, while some small dinosaurs had wings and could fly.

A: You might think it was the *T. rex*, but the *Argentinosaurus* was much bigger. It may have measured up to 130 ft (40 m) long—more than three times longer than a *T. rex*. It was a herbivore and walked on four legs.

A: Paleontologists like me study fossils. Some show more than bone—they tell us about skin and muscles. Birds are *living* dinosaurs, too, so that helps us work out what some dinosaurs may have looked and behaved like.

A: The nonbird dinosaurs suddenly became extinct about 66 million years ago. Many scientists believe that a huge asteroid must have hit Earth, causing a mass extinction and wiping out these dinosaurs.

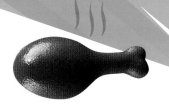

T. rex had about 60 sharp, bone-crunching teeth. Some were about 12 in (30 cm) long.

CHOMP!

This hungry carnivore could easily swallow small dinosaurs whole!

GULP.

T. rex lived in what is now the

USA
and
Canada.

TYRANNOSAURUS REX

tie-RAN-oh-SAW-russ rex

4 m
3 m
2 m
1 m

From toe to hip, a *T. rex* grew up to 13 ft (4 m) tall! The average worldwide height for men is only 5 ft 7 in (1.71 m) tall.

Roar! *Tyrannosaurus rex* (*T. rex*) was a fearsome and ferocious predator. Its name means "tyrant lizard king," and its super senses made it one of the deadliest animals of all time. This mighty beast could eat an enormous *Triceratops* for breakfast!

DR. WU'S DINOSAURS

Jurassic Park's *T. rex* is slightly longer than a real-life version at 44 ft 4 in (13.5 m), and weighs more at 18,518 lb (8,400 kg). She has moderate intelligence, can run at 32 mph (52 kph), and is 17 ft 1 in (5.2 m) in height.

DINO FILES

Length

43 ft (13 m)

Weight
15,432 lb (7,000 kg)

Top speed
20 mph (32 kph)

Intelligence
Pretty smart, but not the cleverest dino ever

HOW TO CATCH A T. REX

Outsmarting Jurassic Park's giant

The *T. rex* is big, fierce, and actually rather smart. You certainly don't want her on the loose, that's for sure! If she does happen to escape though, she can be captured with a little bit of cunning and the right equipment. You might need a bit of courage, too!

1

Prepare the dino cage, ready to trap the *T. rex*.

2

Use a motorcycle to track the *T. rex* and get her attention. Then drive really fast toward the cage.

3

Near the cage, fire the trap shooter and lasso the *T. rex*'s leg.

4

Lead the *T. rex* to the cage. GOOD WORK!

VELOCIRAPTOR

vel-OSS-uh-rap-tor

Boasting high intelligence and super-sharp claws, *Velociraptor* lived between 71–75 million years ago. This cunning carnivore moved fast on two legs— hunting small lizards, mammals, and even other dinosaurs!

A long, stiff tail helped *Velociraptor* steer while running.

Velociraptor was closely related to birds (a bit like a distant cousin) and also laid its eggs in nests.

DINO FILES

Length

6 ft 7 in (2 m)

Weight

33 lb (15 kg)

Top speed

25 mph (40 kph)

Intelligence

Velociraptor was one of the smartest dinosaurs.

25 mph (40 kph)

30 mph (48 kph)

Velociraptor was slower than you think. Your pet cat could actually run faster!

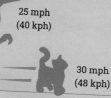

DR. WU'S DINOSAURS

Dr. Wu creates a *Raptor* for Jurassic World that is nearly 20% bigger than the original *Raptors* at Jurassic Park—and almost twice the length and over 13 times heavier than a real-life *Raptor*!

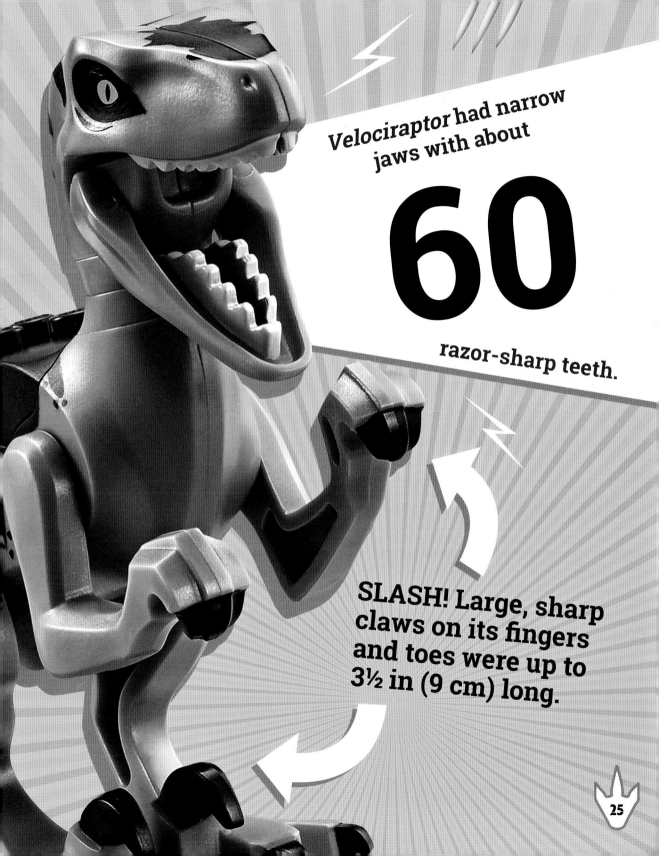

Velociraptor had narrow jaws with about

60

razor-sharp teeth.

SLASH! Large, sharp claws on its fingers and toes were up to 3½ in (9 cm) long.

Top secret!
The cold storage unit contains dinosaur DNA and embryos. If these materials get into the wrong hands, anyone could make their own dinosaurs!

PUUUUSH!
That *Raptor* must not get in!

COME ON, I CAN DO THIS!

The computer controls the park's power supply. If Lex can figure out how the computer works, she can restore the power and call for help.

THE CONTROL ROOM

Jurassic Park's nerve center

The power is down in the park and the *Velociraptor* dinos are on the loose! The best place to be might be the computer control room, with its strong walls and a lockable door. Alan, Ellie, Lex, and Tim will be safe here. Won't they?!

Don't panic, Tim! The kitchen cabinet is a great place to hide!

Everyone needs to help out!

LEGEND OF ISLA NUBLAR

Okay, so things didn't go so well at Jurassic Park. But that doesn't mean that a dinosaur theme park isn't an EXCELLENT idea! New owner Simon Masrani has bigger dinos, better attractions, and a great team working for him. Claire Dearing, the Assistant Manager, is smart and organized, while Owen Grady is an expert *Raptor* trainer. **Come visit Jurassic World!**

CLAIRE DEARING

Determined and devoted Assistant Manager

Claire started out at Jurassic World as an intern after college. She soon impressed the park's boss, Simon Masrani, with her ability to handle tricky situations. Claire works hard, and her aim is to manage the whole park one day. She's got this!

NO PROBLEM, I CAN FIX THIS!

Claire has loved animals since she was a child.

Varied job

Claire makes sure that the dinos are safe and the guests are happy. She even helps out in the lab if needed. Claire loves her job!

Fantastic new idea!

Simon has endless new ideas for the park—from zany rides to a whopping 36 mile (58 km) safari. Even Claire struggles to keep up with him!

Dino buddy

Claire knows that the dinosaurs are the stars of the park. She likes to spend time with the baby *Raptors* and check in on their training.

Teamwork

Claire often teams up with her colleague, Owen. They don't always agree about the best way of doing things, but somehow they get the job done!

WHO'S WHO

Life is never dull at Jurassic World! There are exciting rides; amazing attractions; and, of course, super-cool dinosaurs. But things don't always go to plan. Come and meet some of the folks who always seem to end up in some crazy adventure.

HUDSON HARPER

MOM, DAD, CAN WE STAY LONGER?

Age: 7 **Job:** Park guest

Most likely to: Wander off and get snatched by a dino.

Even more likely to: Get mixed up with a secret plot.

RED THE DOG

WOOF! WOOF! WOOF!

Job: Owen Grady's loyal sidekick

Likes: Owen, of course. They go way back.

Skills: Helping Owen round up escaped *Dilophosauruses*.

DR. ALLISON MILES

I KNOW WHAT I'M DOING!

Job: Dr. Wu's assistant

Likes: Dinosaurs; DNA; doing the right thing (eventually).

Dislikes: Dr. Wu deleting her brilliant work by mistake.

SIMON MASRANI

*LET'S MAKE A **TALKING** GARBAGE CAN!*

Job: Billionaire park owner

Most likely to: Come up with brilliant (crazy) ideas.

Least likely to: Worry; take "no" for an answer.

ACU TROOPER

*WE'VE GOT A **SITUATION** HERE!*

Job: Asset Containment

That means: Making sure the dinos stay in their paddocks.

He has to: Keep guests safe; round up any loose dinos.

VIC HOSKINS

*T. REX ON THE LOOSE? **ZAP IT!***

Job: Head of Park Security

Most likely to: Try and zap anything that gets in his way.

Top secret: Vic is scared of bugs and dinosaurs!

PARK WORKER

*UH, I THINK IT'S **CLOSING** TIME!*

Job: Selling popcorn

Most likely to: Get chased by an escaped dino.

Least likely to: Come back to work tomorrow.

MARKET STALL

Treats and gifts for any dino fan

Jurassic World has everything any dino-loving guest could want. Hudson Harper thinks it's awesome! But the park worker might have spotted something ...

I'LL HAVE A BUCKET OF DINO-CORN PLEASE.

POP

Its upper horns were up to 3 ft 3 in (1 m) long, and its bony neck frill was as wide as the horns were long.

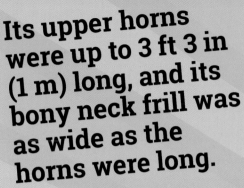

DR. WU'S DINOSAURS

Jurassic World's *Triceratops* dinos are a tiny bit shorter than real-life versions were, at 29 ft 2 in (8.9 m) long. Dr. Wu's dinos also weigh more at 20,000 lb (9,072 kg), and are less intelligent.

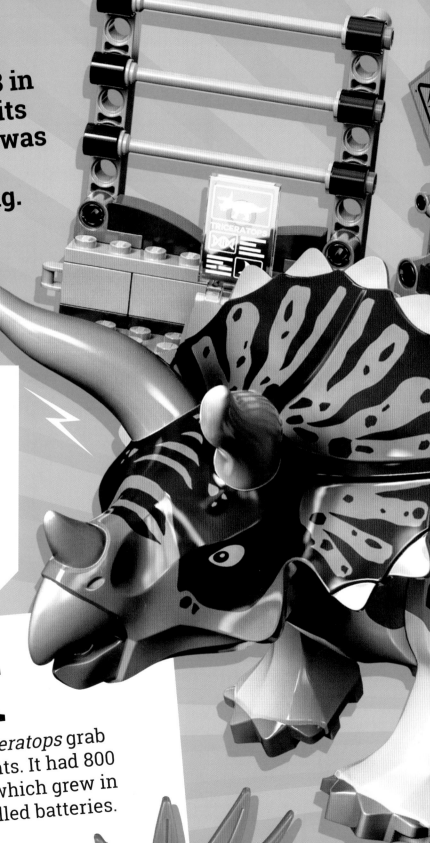

This large, parrotlike

BEAK

helped *Triceratops* grab tougher plants. It had 800 little teeth, which grew in columns called batteries.

TRICERATOPS

try-SAIR-uh-tops

BEHIND YOU!

Fossil evidence shows *T. rex* preyed on *Triceratops*.

This enormous herbivore lived about 70 million years ago in what is now the USA and Canada. *Triceratops* is easy to recognize thanks to its big, bony neck frill and three horns. In fact, its name means "three-horned face" in ancient Greek.

DINO FILES

Length

30 ft (9 m)

Weight

17,637 lb (8,000 kg)

Top speed

25 mph (40 kph)

Intelligence

Triceratops was of average intelligence.

1m 2m 3m 4m 5m 6m 7m 8m 9m 10m

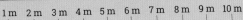

Triceratops was up to 30 ft (9 m) long. That's longer than a garbage truck! But *Triceratops* was probably less smelly.

EGG SPINNER RIDE

Take a spin on the "Scrambler"

This ride is eggs-tremely awesome! Take a seat in a giant dino egg and hold on tight. As it spins, it's soon clear why it's nicknamed the "Scrambler"! The ride is designed for kids, but adults love it, too.

Sorry, this ride is just for humans!

Keep out!

The ride is surrounded by an electrified fence to keep any curious dinosaurs out. Dr. Miles waves to the *Triceratops*, who just seems a bit confused by it all!

Modeled on incubators in the Hammond Creation Lab

IN A SPIN
The ride turns so fast that eating ice cream while on board is not recommended. This visitor may end up wearing her chocolate cone ...

SPIN ME AGAIN, I LOVE THIS RIDE!

39

OWEN GRADY

Animal behaviorist and dino trainer

Owen Grady likes to be at the center of the action. He used to be in the US Navy and is great at building and fixing things. He loves animals and finds it easy to connect with and understand dinosaurs. But relating to people is harder!

I'M ON IT! LET'S GO.

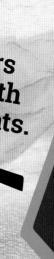

Owen carries canisters filled with dino treats.

High flier

Owen usually rides a motorcycle, but he also flies planes and drives offroaders. Delta the *Velociraptor* loves to come along for the ride.

No fear

Owen feels comfortable around animals. Even a large, angry *Baryonyx* dinosaur doesn't scare him. Owen figures out that this dino is just hungry.

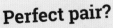

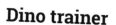

Perfect pair?

Owen probably wouldn't admit it, but he likes Claire a lot. They often argue, but they still have amazing adventures together.

Dino trainer

No one thought that *Raptors* could be trained, until Owen came along! The baby *Raptors* respond to the dinosaur trainer's commands.

41

FAMILY ALBUM

Cute, curious, and a bit mischievous

The *Velociraptor* babies picked Owen as their alpha (leader) and will follow his commands. Well, most of the time. They're just kids, so they don't always do what they're told. But, aw, look how cute they are!

Blue

Blue is the beta (second-in-command). She's the oldest and smartest *Raptor* and adores Owen.

Delta

Delta is the second oldest member of the pack. She backs up Blue whenever she needs it.

Echo

The third *Raptor*, Echo, wishes that she was the boss. This sometimes leads her to fight with Blue.

Charlie

The youngest of the *Raptors*, Charlie, follows where her sisters lead. Most of the time.

I CAN DO SOME GREAT WORK WITH THESE RAPTORS. HEY, COME BACK HERE!

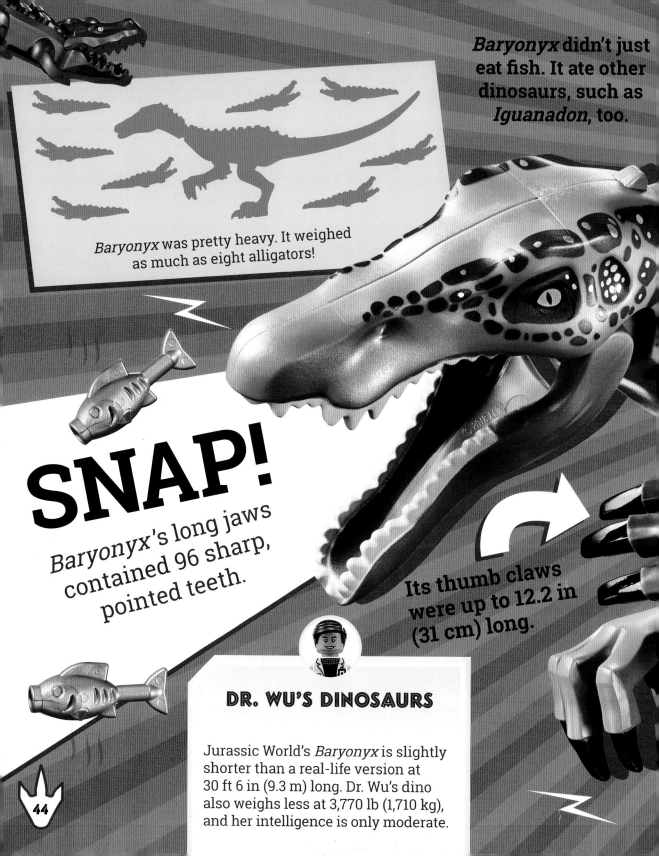

Baryonyx didn't just eat fish. It ate other dinosaurs, such as *Iguanadon*, too.

Baryonyx was pretty heavy. It weighed as much as eight alligators!

SNAP!

Baryonyx's long jaws contained 96 sharp, pointed teeth.

Its thumb claws were up to 12.2 in (31 cm) long.

DR. WU'S DINOSAURS

Jurassic World's *Baryonyx* is slightly shorter than a real-life version at 30 ft 6 in (9.3 m) long. Dr. Wu's dino also weighs less at 3,770 lb (1,710 kg), and her intelligence is only moderate.

BARYONYX

bah-ree-ON-icks

Baryonyx is closely related to the
ENORMOUS
predator *Spinosaurus*.

Snap! Snap! *Baryonyx* used its crocodilelike jaws to grab fish to eat. It also had a huge thumb claw, which it used to hook and stab fish. In fact, the name *Baryonyx* means "heavy claw."

DINO FILES

Length
32 ft 10 in (10 m)

Weight
4,400 lb (2,000 kg)

Top speed
20 mph (32 kph)

Intelligence
Nearly top of the class, but not quite.

TREASURE HUNTERS

Bad guys doing bad things, badly

Danny Nedermeyer works in technology at Jurassic World. He is secretly plotting to ruin the park! Adventurer Sinjin Prescott is helping Danny, for a price. He's been hired to track down some treasure. Danny plans to sell it and start a new, even better park!

Treasure expert

Sinjin Prescott is searching Isla Nublar for the lost treasure of the legendary Captain No Beard. He doesn't care whose treasure it is—it's just an awesome adventure!

Family secrets

Danny Nedermeyer's uncle, Dennis Nedry, helped bring down the original Jurassic Park. Danny is just continuing his uncle's (bad) work.

So close!

Dennis Nedry left details on an old videotape of where to find the hidden treasure. Danny must watch it before the *Baryonyx* catches him.

Sinjin always carries a backpack with emergency snacks.

HEY! WHERE'S MY HAT? IT'S MY FAVORITE.

I'LL BUY YOU A NEW ONE WHEN WE SELL THE TREASURE!

Danny wears his favorite Hawaiian shirt.

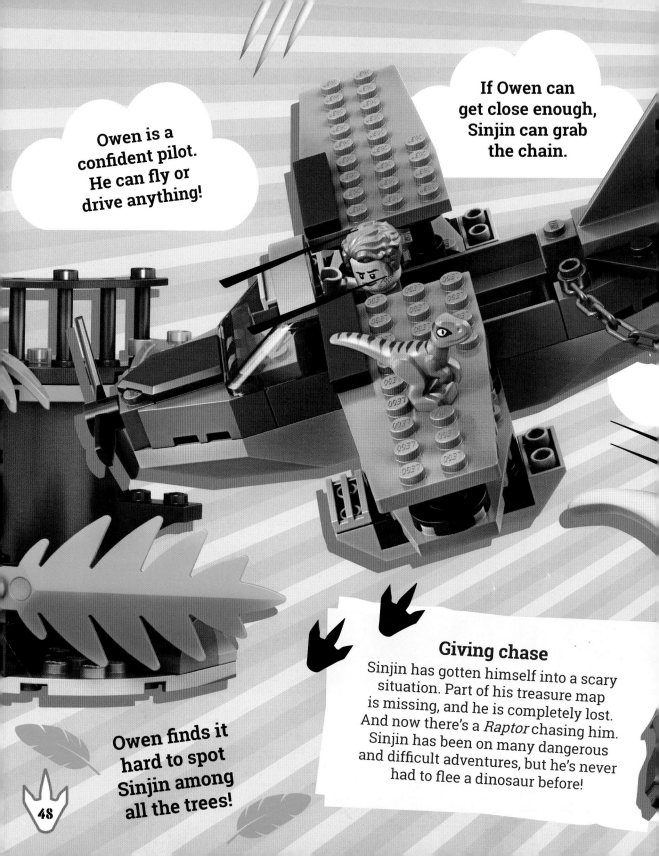

RESCUE MISSION

Good guy rescues a bad guy

Sinjin Prescott has gotten a bit lost in Isla Nublar's jungles. Fortunately, Owen Grady is on his way to rescue him. But can Owen reach Sinjin before an escaped *Raptor* catches him? And will Owen discover what cunning Sinjin is really up to?

This *Raptor* is fast. And hungry!

AAARGH! DON'T LET THAT RAPTOR CATCH ME!

The gem is sparkling in the sun—maybe Owen will spot it!

This excellent sprinter was among the fastest of all the dinosaurs. It was also about as

FAST

as a racehorse!

Although feathers haven't been found on *Gallimimus* yet, experts think it was covered in them like other members of its family.

Gallimimus was twice as tall as an adult human.

Gallimimus weighed the same as about

50

large chickens!

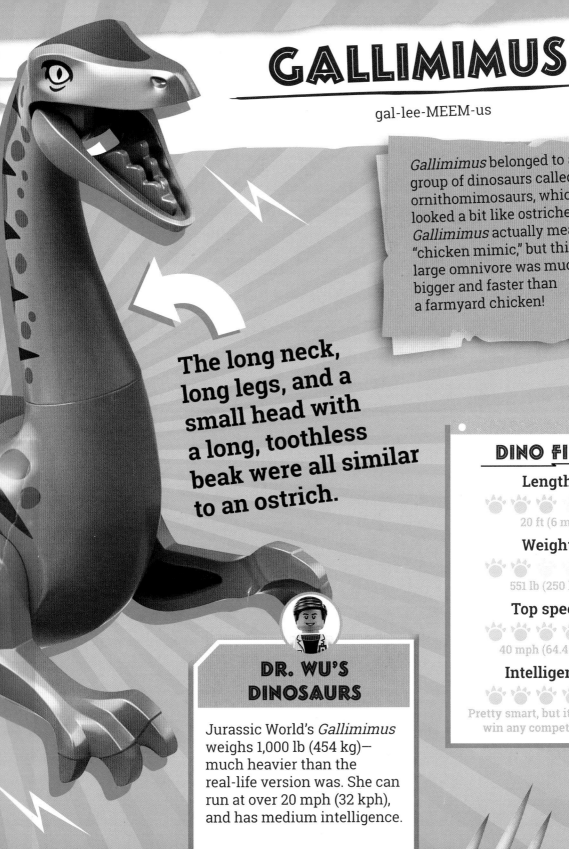

GALLIMIMUS

gal-lee-MEEM-us

Gallimimus belonged to a group of dinosaurs called ornithomimosaurs, which all looked a bit like ostriches. *Gallimimus* actually means "chicken mimic," but this large omnivore was much bigger and faster than a farmyard chicken!

The long neck, long legs, and a small head with a long, toothless beak were all similar to an ostrich.

DINO FILES

Length
20 ft (6 m)

Weight
551 lb (250 kg)

Top speed
40 mph (64.4 kph)

Intelligence
Pretty smart, but it might not win any competitions ...

DR. WU'S DINOSAURS

Jurassic World's *Gallimimus* weighs 1,000 lb (454 kg)—much heavier than the real-life version was. She can run at over 20 mph (32 kph), and has medium intelligence.

The net shooter has been deployed.

Extra feature
The research vehicle has two detachable drones. They can explore places that this mighty vehicle can't reach.

Huge tires can handle most terrain.

93

RESEARCH VEHICLE

Fully equipped and ready for action

The cockpit has space for two people.

This sturdy vehicle has everything Claire needs to study dinosaurs on the move, including a mini laboratory. It also has some extra tools that might come in handy if any of the dinos get loose.

On the run

This escaped *Gallimimus* can't get away. With the push of a button, Claire fires the net shooter. Gotcha!

54

DOUBLE TROUBLE

Pteranodon and *Gallimimus* on the loose

When a *Pteranodon* and a *Gallimimus* break free, the chase is on! They are two of the fastest creatures at Jurassic World.

CAW! CAW!

HELP! I NEED BACKUP IMMEDIATELY!

DR. WU'S DINOSAURS

Dr. Wu's *Dilophosaurus* dinos have moderate intelligence and so they are not quite as smart as real-life versions were. But one Jurassic Park *Dilophosaurus* does take a strong dislike to bad guy Dennis Nedry, so she must be bright!

Dilophosaurus weighed as much as a horse, but it was much fiercer!

DINO FILES

Length

23 ft (7 m)

Weight

1,102 lb (500 kg)

Top speed

22 mph (35.4 kph)

Intelligence

Slightly less smart than a *Velociraptor*.

Dilophosaurus moved on two feet and its large tail helped it balance.

Fossils of *Dilophosaurus* have only been found in the USA and are from the Jurassic Period, around 190 million years ago.

DILOPHOSAURUS

die-LOAF-oh-saw-us

Two bony crests on the top of its head made this dino stand out from others. It's not known what it used the crests for—but scientists think it was to attract mates and perhaps just to show off. It was one of the largest meat-eating dinosaurs of its day!

Dilophosaurus ate plant-eating dinos and other animals, probably including fish.

CRUNCH!

SNATCH!
Dilophosaurus was fast and used its claws to slash at its prey before biting them.

Cool features

The drone's sensors can track the location of dinosaurs. It also has a net, which can shoot out and stop any escaped dinos.

The drone is powered by four spinning rotors.

58

DRONE HELICOPTER

Great for scanning remote corners of the island

Owen can pilot the drone from its built-in cockpit.

Jurassic World has all the latest technology, including this drone helicopter. It's fast and light, and it can be controlled remotely—ideal for patrolling the far reaches of Isla Nublar.

Cameras send information back to the control room.

Park patrol
The only thing that might get in the way of a flying drone is a curious flying *Pteranodon*! When the drone finishes a trip, it returns to its rectangular landing pad.

T. REX VS. DINO MECH

Dinosaur vs. dino robot

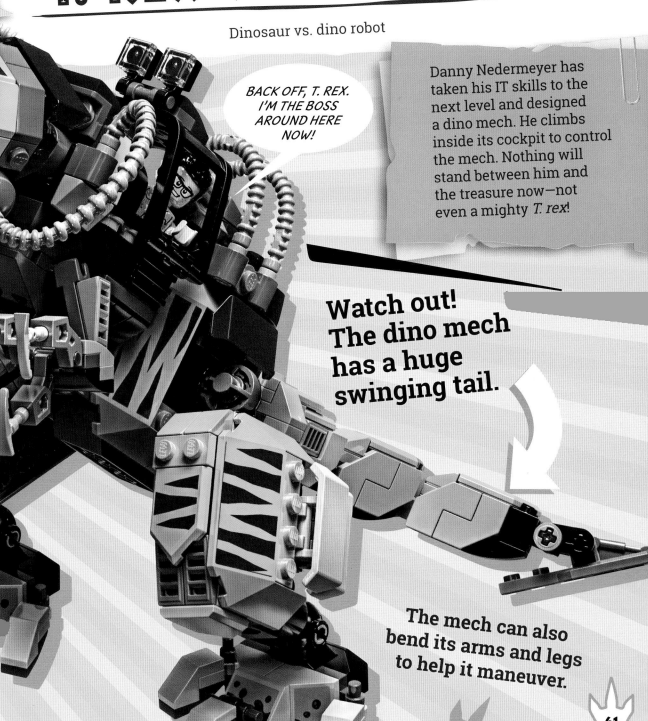

BACK OFF, T. REX. I'M THE BOSS AROUND HERE NOW!

Danny Nedermeyer has taken his IT skills to the next level and designed a dino mech. He climbs inside its cockpit to control the mech. Nothing will stand between him and the treasure now—not even a mighty *T. rex*!

Watch out! The dino mech has a huge swinging tail.

The mech can also bend its arms and legs to help it maneuver.

BIPLANE

Flying search and rescue vehicle

One of the perks of working at Jurassic World is getting to try out all sorts of awesome vehicles. Owen can't pick a favorite, but this cool biplane is certainly one of the best. Time to be a hero!

Delta is secretly enjoying the trip.

Easy landing

This biplane has a really cool feature—it can land on water! Floats beneath the wings ensure a smooth landing if Owen needs to touch down on the ocean.

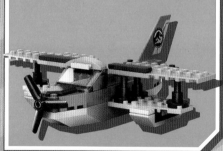

The chain can be lowered to haul up stranded people to safety.

Biplanes have two pairs of wings.

Watch out for the spinning propeller!

Plan B
All-action Owen also has a tough offroader vehicle on standby. Its big tires can cope with the rocky terrain of Isla Nublar. Wherever a missing person is, Owen will find them.

Even an angry *T. rex* would be no match for a raging volcano!

MOUNT SIBO

A dormant volcano (or is it?)

Uh-oh. This lava does look pretty fresh!

If dangerous dinosaurs aren't enough to worry about, Isla Nublar is also home to an enormous volcano. Mount Sibo hasn't erupted for centuries though. Surely there's plenty of time left before it explodes?

Treasure!
It's not just hot rocks inside this volcano—it's hiding a treasure chest stuffed full of gold and jewels. Whoever finds it would be rich beyond their wildest dreams.

MY SINISTER PLAN IS GOING SO WELL!

JURASSIC WORLD

Jurassic World's boss, Simon Masrani, always wants to improve his park and create spectacular new sights. The more extreme, the better! He is demanding a new attraction to make Jurassic World the best ever theme park. It's got to be something unique—big, exciting, and a little scary. **Dr. Wu has a plan. What could possibly go wrong?**

MANAGING EVERYTHING

Keeping Jurassic World running smoothly

Claire now has her dream job as director of park operations at Jurassic World. She's in charge of running the park—a big responsibility. It's what she worked so hard for, but it doesn't leave much time for friends or family.

Too busy

Claire hasn't seen her nephews Zach and Gray for a few years, and even now that they're visiting the park, she doesn't have much time for them. She's got to work!

In the action

Claire is brave and decisive. If a dinosaur escapes, she'll step in and help the Asset Containment Unit (ACU) track the dino down.

Bold leader

Jurassic World's staffers look to Claire to tell them what to do. She is calm and confident in her important role.

WHO'S WHO

It takes a lot of different people to keep Jurassic World running smoothly. Some focus on looking after the animals, while others work in safety and security. Some, like Simon Masrani, just want to put on an awesome show for the park guests without worrying too much about safety. Uh-oh ...

OWEN GRADY

*I'M THE **ALPHA** AROUND HERE!*

Job: Animal behaviorist

Most likely to: Act without thinking (but it kind of works).

Least likely to: Make a plan or talk about his feelings.

SIMON MASRANI

*YOU SEEM A LITTLE **STRESSED**, CLAIRE!*

Job: Billionaire park owner

Most likely to: Ignore advice; fly a helicopter (badly).

Least likely to: Listen; think things through properly.

ACU TROOPER

*I THINK WE'RE GOING TO NEED **BACKUP!***

Job: Asset Containment

Best part of job: The excitement of seeing a brand-new dinosaur.

Worst part of job: Facing off with grumpy dinos.

ACU TROOPER

*THERE'S A **T. REX** ON THE LOOSE!*

Job: Asset Containment

Likes: Being right in the middle of the action.

Dislikes: Dinos getting a little too close ...

PALEOVETERINARIAN

*THAT **DINOSAUR** NEEDS MY HELP!*

Job: Caring for sick dinos

Dislikes: Having to catch dinos before treating them.

Never seen without: His lucky fedora.

VIC HOSKINS

*I'M **IN CHARGE** HERE NOW!*

Job: Head of Park Security

Would like to: Turn *Raptors* into soldiers. (Bad idea!)

Did you know? He used to have a pet wolf.

BARRY SEMBÈNE

*VIC, THAT RAPTOR IS **HUNGRY** ...*

Job: *Raptor* trainer

Favorite dino: Delta (shhh, don't tell the others).

Fun fact: Barry is an old friend of Owen's.

71

DR. HENRY WU

Lead genetic biologist and head of the Hammond Creation Lab

Dr. Wu is an expert in genes—the parts of cells that determine a creature's characteristics. He's a great scientist. There's just one problem: he's not worried about how his ideas might turn out in the real world!

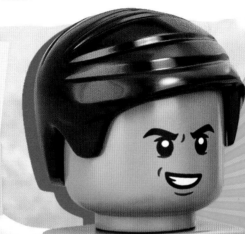

WHAT DANGEROUS DINO?! NOT MY PROBLEM ...

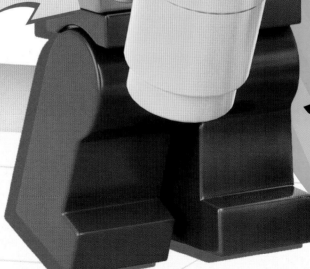

Brilliant minds need lots of coffee!

Babysitter

The worst part of Dr. Wu's job is feeding the newly hatched dino babies. They get so cranky when they're hungry!

High tech

Dr. Wu has expensive computers and incubators in his lab. He had better not spill his coffee!

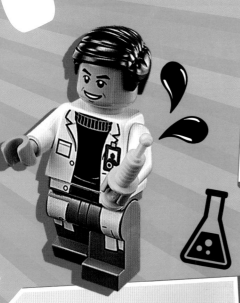

Closer look

Dr. Wu examines tiny cells with his microscope. Every little detail is important in his work.

Emergency!

The medicine in Dr. Wu's syringe helps calm dangerous dinos, if he can catch them!

73

CREATING DINOSAURS

Inside the Hammond Creation Lab at Jurassic World

In the lab, Dr. Wu and his team use dinosaur DNA to make dino eggs. The eggs hatch into baby dinosaurs. It's always busy in the lab. Today, the park alarm goes off as a baby *Triceratops* breaks out of her cage!

DNA is a blueprint, or set of instructions, for building a living thing.

THAT WASN'T SUPPOSED TO HAPPEN!

Eggs are **incubated**, or kept warm, until the baby dinosaurs are ready to hatch.

Screens flash with urgent information for Dr. Wu!

Dr. Wu gives water to the thirsty baby *Ankylosaurus*. He likes to keep a close eye on the newly hatched dinosaurs.

Dr. Wu's guide to creating dinosaurs:

1) Find a fully preserved, blood-sucking mosquito that lived among the dinos.
2) Extract blood containing dino DNA from the mosquito.
3) Use the DNA to create dinosaur embryos and eggs.
4) Wait for the baby dinos to hatch!

ZACH & GRAY MITCHELL

Brothers on the vacation of a lifetime!

Zach and Gray have very different personalities. Older brother Zach is cool and calm, while Gray is chatty and enthusiastic. Gray is a dinosaur fan and can't wait to explore Jurassic World, but Zach isn't interested in much apart from his cell phone!

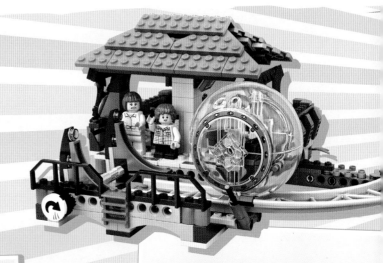

Best time

Gray has fun exploring Jurassic World. He loves getting close to the dinos in a Gyrosphere. Gray is glad his big brother is around when things start to go wrong.

Family reunion?

Gray and Zach's parents send them to Jurassic World to visit their aunt, Claire. But Claire is too busy running the park to hang out with them.

Too close!

Zach will protect his little brother from anything—even a dangerous Indominus rex! If a dino gets too close, Zach's calm head and quick thinking can get the pair out of harm's way.

Pteranodon hunted at sea, swimming on the ocean surface like a seabird and diving down to catch

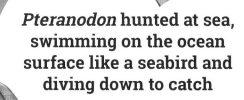

FISH!

BIRD'S-EYE VIEW
Pteranodon's particularly large eyes helped it spot food, like fast fish.

Using its long, narrow wings, *Pteranodon* soared across oceans and seas, only occasionally flapping its wings.

Pteranodon had three movable fingers with sharp claws at the bend of each wing.

Their long jaws looked similar to a pelican's and had no teeth.

PTERANODON

teh-RAN-uh-don

Swoosh! The fascinating *Pteranodon* was not actually a dinosaur—it was a flying reptile that belonged to a group known as pterosaurs. *Pteranodon* had a distinctive, long crest on its head that pointed backward.

1m 2m 3m 4m 5m 6m 7m

Pteranodon had a wingspan of more than 23 ft (7 m)—that's nearly three times wider than a bald eagle's wingspan at 6–8 ft (1.8–2.4 m).

DINO FILES

Wingspan
23 ft (7 m)

Weight
77 lb (35 kg)

Top speed
70 mph (112.7 kph)

Intelligence
Not your average "bird brain."

DR. WU'S PTERANODON

A Jurassic World *Pteranodon* is heavier than a real-life version at 125 lb (57 kg), and also a bit less intelligent. She is 7 ft (2.1 m) long from beak to tail.

79

Large spinning rotor blades

In the net!
Gotcha! The net shooter works, but the *Pteranodon* may have damaged the helicopter's blades. Flying in a straight line is even harder now!

MAYBE I SHOULD HAVE HAD A FEW MORE FLYING LESSONS!

Simon Masrani just got his pilot's license.

HELICOPTER

A bumpy ride on the *Jurassic One*

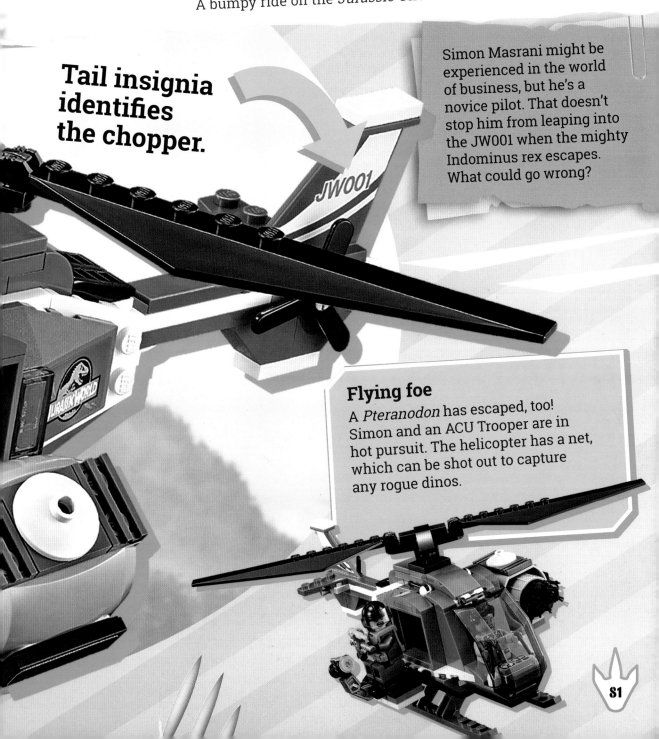

Tail insignia identifies the chopper.

JW001

Simon Masrani might be experienced in the world of business, but he's a novice pilot. That doesn't stop him from leaping into the JW001 when the mighty Indominus rex escapes. What could go wrong?

Flying foe

A *Pteranodon* has escaped, too! Simon and an ACU Trooper are in hot pursuit. The helicopter has a net, which can be shot out to capture any rogue dinos.

ANKYLOSAURUS

an-KIE-loh-saw-us

Don't mess with an *Ankylosaurus*! This big, tough herbivore was built like a tank. Its thick, bony armor protected it from the sharp teeth and claws of meat eaters, such as *T. rex*.

1m 2m 3m 4m 5m 6m 7m 8m 9m

Ankylosaurus was up to 30 ft (9 m) long. That's longer than the width of three school buses!

DINO FILES

Length

30 ft (9 m)

Weight

13,228 lb (6,000 kg)

Top speed

6 mph (9.7 kph)

Intelligence

Ankylosaurus was all about brawn, not brains.

Ankylosaurus weighed almost as much as

THREE
RHINOCEROSES!

At the end of this dino's tail was a huge, bony mass which formed a hard club. The club was great for swinging at predators!

DR. WU'S DINOSAURS

The *Ankylosaurus* Dr. Wu designs for Jurassic World is heavier than a real-life version at 17,600 lb (7,983 kg). She is also a little bit longer at 31 ft 6 in (9.6 m).

DO NOT DISTURB!

As well as its bony armor, *Ankylosaurus* also had spikes along its body and small horns on its head.

Ankylosaurus ate by grinding plants with its teeth. It had a large gut to help it digest food. Some ankylosaurs have been found with their last meal inside their belly.

GYROSPHERE

Rolling with the herds

The coolest way for visitors to explore the park is in a Gyrosphere. These glass balls roll at gentle speeds of up to 5 mph (8 kph), allowing guests to observe herds of *Ankylosaurus* or *Triceratops* in action.

Glass is tough enough to withstand a bullet, but not the Indominus rex's claws.

Backup plan
The Gyrospheres are very safe, but ACU Troopers also patrol the area in their offroaders. But, really, what could possibly go wrong?

Built-in computer identifies nearby dinos.

HELP, I THINK
I'M LOST!

Security

Invisible fences keep the dinos from roaming too far. If a dino does escape, ACU Troopers are ready to stop and redirect any strays—or transport them back to their padddocks.

The door is locked tight to keep guests safe.

DINO PADDOCK

Keeping the park's newest attraction safe

Dr. Wu has created a new type of dinosaur. Named the Indominus rex, no one is sure what she can do. One thing is obvious: she's BIG. She needs a secure paddock until Claire and the team work out how to handle her.

Eye in the sky

An ACU Trooper checks on the Indominus rex from a helicopter. Bad news! She appears to be escaping. Red alert! This dino needs to be rounded up fast.

HELP! I THINK SHE'S COMING AFTER ME!

SCREEECH!

Despite the tall walls and high-tech security in her paddock, the Indominus rex has escaped. She's free for the first time ever! What will she do?

The observation tower gives Dr. Wu a great view of the chaos.

DINOSAUR SHOWDOWN!

Scary new carnivore vs. tough, armored herbivore

The Indominus rex has escaped! And she's definitely not looking to make friends with this *Ankylosaurus ...*

Trap door can be activated quickly if the *Raptors* try to escape.

The paddock has a secure electric fence.

RAPTOR PADDOCK

At home with the cunning carnivores

The paddock is well lit so the *Raptors* can't hide.

Echo and Charlie are safe and secure in their paddock. It is not yet open to the public, as Owen Grady and Barry Sembène are still training them. They know the *Raptors* pretty well, but the dinos can still surprise them ...

Prepared

Barry's job is to care for the *Raptors*. He can tell if they're hungry or scared. But he still carries a tranquilizer dart, in case they attack.

HOW ABOUT A LITTLE SNACK BEFORE YOUR CHECK-UP?

A paleoveterinarian gives the *Raptors* regular check-ups.

RAPTOR RAMPAGE

Blue and Delta are running free!

Uh-oh! The *Raptors* have gotten loose and they might attack the mobile vet unit. The vehicle is not built to withstand the *Raptors'* sharp claws. Fortunately, Owen is keeping up with the dinos on his motorcycle. Can he get them safely back to their paddock?

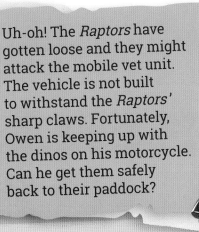

Delta is able to run wherever she wants for the first time.

Blue doesn't want to listen to Owen. This is too much fun!

FINDING FREEDOM

Angry Indominus rex on the loose

The Indominus rex has spent her entire life in labs or paddocks, but now she's free for the first time. And she's pretty mad! She's not going to let anything stand in her way—Gyrospheres, trees, or even other dinos. Owen must try his best to stop her!

The Indominus rex tricked humans to escape. She has camouflage abilities!

The Indominus rex's roar is as loud as a jet plane on takeoff.

94

She doesn't go around obstacles. She just knocks them down!

WHAT EXACTLY IS THIS CREATURE?!

Amazing creation

The Indominus rex was created by Dr. Wu. She is a hybrid—a mix of different species. Dr. Wu used genes from many dinos plus other creatures (such as tree frogs) to create her. She has different skills thanks to all these different genes. Owen may need some help to outsmart her!

95

JURASSIC WORLD: FALLEN KINGDOM

After the Indominus rex's breakout, Jurassic World is in ruins. The humans have left and the other dinos are roaming freely on Isla Nublar. But Mount Sibo is about to erupt, and the dinos are in danger. However, not everyone has the dinosaurs' best interests at heart. **Maybe a volcano is not the biggest danger these dinos are facing ...**

HURRY! WE MUST SAVE THESE DINOSAURS.

WHO'S WHO

Everyone has a different view on what is best for the dinosaurs. Claire forms the Dinosaur Protection Group (DPG) to help keep dinos safe and to fight for their rights. Many people agree with her, but others see dinosaurs as a way to make money—or as a danger that must be stopped.

ZIA RODRIGUEZ

REAL DINOSAURS? I'VE GOT TO GET CLOSER!

Job: DPG's paleoveterinarian

What's that? She's a vet for dinosaurs.

She would: Risk her life to save a sick *T. rex.*

FRANKLIN WEBB

AAARGH! I AM NOT READY FOR THIS!

Job: DPG's technology genius

Likes: Solving tricky tech problems—they're easy.

Dislikes: Field work. It's safer behind a screen!

MAISIE LOCKWOOD

I'M GOING TO SET THEM FREE.

Age: 9

Lives: In a huge mansion with its own dino museum.

Loves: Dinosaurs, and anyone who loves dinos, too.

DR. HENRY WU

*LOOK WHAT I CAN CREATE! I'M A **GENIUS!***

Job: Head of the dino lab

Most likely to: Create a scary new kind of dinosaur.

Least likely to: Worry about what the dinosaur might do.

ELI MILLS

*I CAN **HELP** YOU, CLAIRE ...*

Job: Businessman; crook

Pretends to: Rescue stranded dinos from Isla Nublar.

Really wants to: Sell dinos to some really bad people.

KEN WHEATLEY

***SAVE** THAT DINOSAUR, OR ELSE!*

Job: Hunter; soldier for hire

Collects: Dinosaur teeth. (This is a really bad idea.)

Cares about: Money. That's it. Just money.

GUNNAR EVERSOL

*WHO'LL BID $10,000,000? **SOLD!***

Job: Auctioneer

What's that? He sells dinos to the highest bidder.

Biggest regret: Getting into an elevator with an Indoraptor.

DINO PROTECTOR

A new Claire with a new mission

Claire was so busy running Jurassic World that she had no time for family or friends. She even lost sight of what was most important—the dinosaurs. But times have changed, and so has Claire. With Jurassic World in ruins, Claire is now focused on helping the dinos left behind.

New mission

Claire has founded the Dinosaur Protection Group. The group believes dinos should not be kept in parks for human entertainment. They deserve protection and to live in peace.

To the rescue

Claire has always been willing to risk her life for others when she needs to. Maisie Lockwood is very grateful for Claire's bravery and quick thinking.

Double act

Claire hasn't seen Owen for a while, but now she needs his help again. She still doesn't always agree with him, but there's no denying that they're a great team!

DINO DECISIONS

What should happen to the dinosaurs on Isla Nublar?

Everyone has different ideas about what's best for the dinosaurs. But one thing's for sure: when Mount Sibo erupts, the whole island will be engulfed in lava, including the dinosaurs. Should they be saved?

PLEASE HELP US RESCUE THEM!

THEY'RE OUT OF OUR CONTROL.

Save them!
Claire and the Dinosaur Protection Group (DPG) believe that dinosaurs have rights. Like any living creature, they deserve a chance to survive.

Leave them!
Dr. Ian Malcolm has always believed that humans cannot control dinosaurs. He thinks they must be left on the island to become extinct again.

BACK IN ACTION

Saving dinosaurs and being a hero. Again.

After the events at Jurassic World, Owen just wanted to be alone. But when Claire needs his help, Owen can't let her down. Especially as his old friend Blue is in trouble, too. Owen is soon back doing what he does best—working alongside Claire to fix things.

Trusty bike

Owen loves his motorcycle. It suits him perfectly—it's fast, cool, and only has room for one!

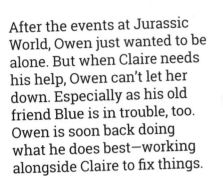

Loyal friend

Owen and Blue go way back, and he'll always look out for her. She saved Owen from the Indominus rex, and now it's his turn to save Blue from Mount Sibo.

A new path

Owen finds that being part of a team is actually pretty awesome. He's getting good at taking care of people, especially Maisie Lockwood.

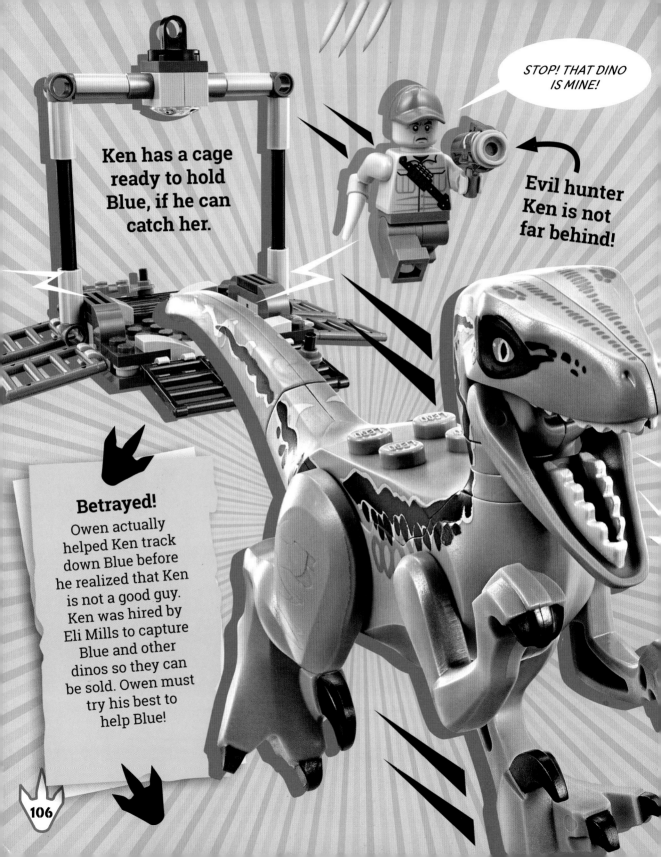

Ken has a cage ready to hold Blue, if he can catch her.

STOP! THAT DINO IS MINE!

Evil hunter Ken is not far behind!

Betrayed!

Owen actually helped Ken track down Blue before he realized that Ken is not a good guy. Ken was hired by Eli Mills to capture Blue and other dinos so they can be sold. Owen must try his best to help Blue!

SAVING AN OLD FRIEND

Owen rides to Blue's rescue

Owen also hopes to save some dino eggs.

COME ON GIRL, I CAN SAVE YOU!

Owen has known Blue since she was a baby. He trained her and watched her grow into an amazing adult dino. Owen hasn't seen Blue since the ruined Jurassic World was closed a few years ago. However, their bond is still very strong.

Owen tries to steer Blue away from Ken Wheatley.

T. REX TRANSPORTER

On the move with a really angry dino

The *T. rex* is being relocated from Isla Nublar, but it's not easy. This transporter has a huge trailer with a mobile containment unit to put her in. But convincing the *T. rex* that going inside is a good idea will be tough!

T. rexes do not like cages!

Medical kit
The *T. rex* is putting up a fight. If she gets injured, she may need a blood transfusion. The transporter has a mobile medical unit on board to make sure the dino stays healthy.

The trailer's side panels are collapsible.

Captured!

The *T. rex* is now secure in the trailer. The high side panels are locked, and long bars keep her in place. It's still wise to keep a safe distance from her though!

Truck and trailer are attached here.

IT'S GOING TO BLOW!

A lava-ly time on Isla Nublar

Things have just gone from bad to really, really bad on Isla Nublar. Franklin, Claire, and Owen are running out of time to save the dinos and themselves. Mount Sibo has started to erupt—and it looks like Ken Wheatley and his ship are leaving without them!

Franklin tries to just roll with it in a Gyrosphere ...

AAARGH! I'M GOING TO GET EATEN OR BURIED IN LAVA!

WE'VE GOT TO GET ON THAT SHIP!

BEING A COOL HERO IS TIRING WORK ...

Kaboom! Mount Sibo has been building up to an eruption for years.

Red-hot lava is spewing out of the volcano. Run!

Stranded!

Owen, Claire, and the DPG have been tricked. Ken was just using them to find the dinos; he was never planning on giving them a ride home afterward. But Claire and Owen have faced worse situations than this. They're all getting off this island!

Carnotaurus had quite small eyes and an oddly shaped skull, so scientists think its sense of smell might have been more important than its eyesight.

Carnotaurus had rows of large bony plates on its side and along its back.

Carnotaurus would have been useless at

CLAPPING.

Its arms were only 1 ft 4 in (0.4 m) long—tiny compared to the rest of its body, and not even long enough to put its hands together or scratch its belly!

CARNOTAURUS

Car-no-TORE-uss

A *Carnotaurus* would lose a race to a hare, which can run up to 50 mph (80 kph).

Ouch! *Carnotaurus* may have used its bull-like horns to head-butt rival dinosaurs. Its name even means "meat-eating bull." *Carnotaurus* was a large, carnivorous dinosaur like *T. rex*, but it was faster. However, even *T. rex* had longer arms!

DINO FILES

Length
30 ft (9 m)

Weight
4,409 lb (2,000 kg)

Top speed
35 mph (56 kph)

Intelligence
Probably quite smart. It's not its fault it can't clap!

DR. WU'S DINOSAURS

Dr. Wu's *Carnotaurus* is slightly longer than a real-life version was and a bit heavier, with only moderate intelligence. She can run faster than the park's *T. rex* thanks to the power in her long back legs.

LOCKWOOD ESTATE

The setting for some epic dinosaur action!

Lockwood Estate is in Northern California. The manor looks grand and elegant, but it hides many dangerous secrets. Ken Wheatley has brought the dinos here from Isla Nublar. It's all part of Eli Mills' wicked scheme ...

The roof wasn't built to hold dinos! It might collapse!

Secret's out!

Dr. Wu has a secret lab at Lockwood and is working on his most terrifying creation yet. The Indoraptor is a hybrid dinosaur and was bred to be a weapon. And now he's on the loose!

I'M COMING TO FIND YOU, MAISIE!

Maisie is trapped in her bedroom. Can Owen get to her in time?

ROOOAR!
The *Velociraptor* is no match for the huge Indoraptor!

115

SHARP BEAK

was used to gather leaves and fruit.

DINO FILES

Length

10 ft (3 m)

Weight
220 lb (100 kg)

Top speed
18 mph (29 kph)

Intelligence
Not the brightest of dinosaurs.

Small hands were useful for collecting food.

STYGIMOLOCH

STIJ-i-MOL-ock

The herbivorous *Stygimoloch* is still a bit of a mystery. Some scientists think it might not even have been a separate species of dinosaur, just the younger form of a large "bonehead" dino called *Pachycephalosaurus*.

Stygimoloch had a smaller dome on its skull than *Pachycephalosaurus*, and much longer horns. It probably rammed other dinosaurs with its bony dome head!

DR. WU'S DINOSAURS

The *Stygimoloch* that Dr. Wu designed for Jurassic World is 11 ft 6 in (3.5 m) long—a little bit longer than the real-life version of this dinosaur was.

This dinosaur stood 4 ft 7 in (1.4 m) tall, a little shorter than the average worldwide height for women at 5 ft 3 in (1.59 m).

2.0 m
1.5 m
1.0 m
0.5 m

BREAKING OUT!

A *Stygimoloch* is on the loose

This *Stygimoloch* might not be the smartest dino, but she knows how to use her head! She is tired of being observed by Dr. Wu in his lab, so she uses her thick skull and horns to bash her way out. Now the guard has to catch her!

OH NO, MY LAB! STOP THAT DINO!

This dino is light and strong. She will be tough to stop!

The dino has smashed a wall and knocked over some eggs.

THE END?

Dinosaurs on the loose

Claire and Owen saved some of the dinosaurs from Eli Mills and his cronies. But now they are roaming freely on the US mainland. What happens now?

121

GLOSSARY

Asset
Something valuable to a business, such as a dinosaur at Jurassic World.

Attractions
Things, such as rides, sights, or animals, that people really want to see or experience.

Behaviorist
An expert who studies behavior: how a person, animal, or plant acts and responds.

Cells
The super-tiny units from which all living things are made.

Characteristics
The qualities or features that something, such as a type of dinosaur, usually has.

DNA (deoxyribonucleic acid)
A substance found in every cell. It determines how a living thing will look and behave.

Embryo
An animal or human that is just starting to develop and has not yet been born or hatched.

Era
A distinct period or time in history.

Genes
The parts of cells that determine a creature's characteristics.

Genetic biologist
A person who studies living organisms, genes, and how they are passed down.

Incubator
A machine that keeps dinosaur eggs warm so they can hatch.

Intern
A student or graduate working at a company, usually for a short time, to gain experience.

Insignia
A symbol or badge showing membership of an organization.

Mech
A robotic suit of armor, usually with a person inside it.

Microscope
A scientific instrument that makes tiny objects look bigger so that the human eye can see them.

Paleobotanist
A person who studies ancient plants.

Paleontologist
A person who studies ancient organisms.

Paleoveterinarian
An expert in the treatment of ancient animals.

Predator
An animal that hunts others for food.

Preserved
Something that is protected from decay.

Prey
An animal that is hunted by others for food.

INDEX

Main entries are in **bold**.

DK | Penguin Random House

Senior Editor Ruth Amos
Senior Designer Thelma-Jane Robb
Project Art Editor Sam Bartlett
Production Editor Marc Staples
Senior Production Controller Lloyd Robertson
US Editor Kayla Dugger
Managing Editor Paula Regan
Managing Art Editor Jo Connor
Publisher Julie Ferris
Art Director Lisa Lanzarini
Publishing Director Mark Searle

Dinosaur Consultant Dr. Dean Lomax

First American Edition, 2021
Published in the United States by DK Publishing
1450 Broadway, Suite 801, New York, NY 10018

Page design copyright © 2021 Dorling Kindersley Limited
DK, a Division of Penguin Random House LLC
21 22 23 24 25   10 9 8 7 6 5 4 3 2 1
001–321865–May/2021

A catalog record for this book
is available from the Library of Congress.
ISBN 978-0-7440-2853-9
978-0-7440-3795-1 (library edition)

DK books are available at special discounts when purchased in bulk for
sales promotions, premiums, fund-raising, or educational use. For details, contact:
DK Publishing Special Markets, 1450 Broadway, Suite 801, New York, NY 10018
SpecialSales@dk.com

Printed and bound in China

For the curious
www.dk.com
www.LEGO.com